Selena the Sleepover Fairy was originally published
as a Rainbow Magic special. This version has
been specially adapted for developing readers
in conjunction with a Reading Consultant.

Special thanks
to Rachel Elliot
and Fiona Munro

Reading Consultant: Prue Goodwin, lecturer in literacy and children's books.

ORCHARD BOOKS

This story first published in Great Britain in 2011 by Orchard Books
First published as an Early Reader in 2014
This edition published in 2019 by The Watts Publishing Group

1 3 5 7 9 10 8 6 4 2

HiT entertainment

© 2019 Rainbow Magic Limited.
© 2019 HIT Entertainment Limited.
Illustrations © Orchard Books 2014

The moral rights of the author and illustrator have been asserted.
All characters and events in this publication, other than those clearly in the public domain,
are fictitious and any resemblance to real persons, living or dead, is purely coincidental.

All rights reserved.
No part of this publication may be reproduced, stored in a retrieval system, or transmitted,
in any form or by any means, without the prior permission in writing of the publisher,
nor be otherwise circulated in any form of binding or cover other than that in which it is
published and without a similar condition including this condition being imposed on the
subsequent purchaser.

A CIP catalogue record for this book is available from the British Library.

ISBN 978 1 40835 982 2

Printed in China

MIX
Paper from
responsible sources
FSC
www.fsc.org
FSC® C104740

The paper and board used in this book are made from wood from responsible sources

Orchard Books
An imprint of Hachette Children's Group
Part of The Watts Publishing Group Limited
Carmelite House, 50 Victoria Embankment, London EC4Y 0DZ

An Hachette UK Company
www.hachette.co.uk
www.hachettechildrens.co.uk